THE PSYCHIC ARTS

PALM READING

BY MEGAN ATWOOD

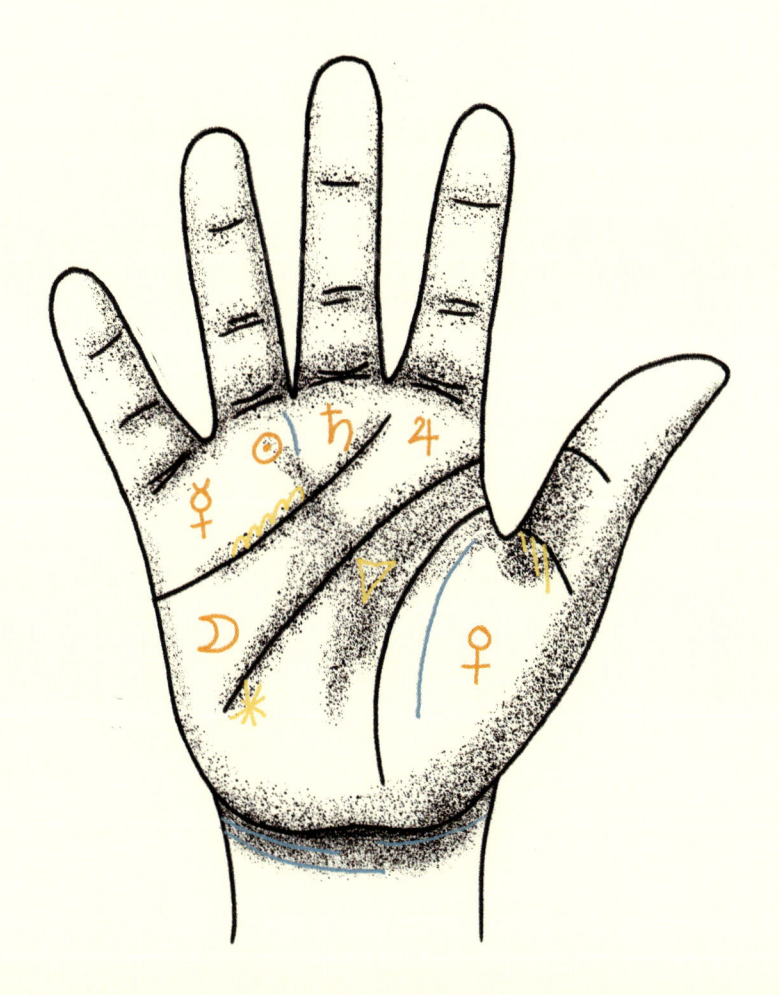

Consultant: Lisa Raggio-Kimmins, M.A., Psychology and Counseling

COMPASS POINT BOOKS
a capstone imprint

Compass Point Books, a Capstone imprint
Psychic Arts is published by Compass Point Books,
1710 Roe Crest Drive, North Mankato, Minnesota, 56003.
www.mycapstone.com

Copyright © 2019 by Capstone Press, a Capstone imprint. All rights reserved. No part of this publication may be reproduced in whole or in part, or stored in a retrieval system, or transmitted in any form or by any means, electronic, mechanical, photocopying, recording, or otherwise, without written permission of the publisher.

Library of Congress Cataloging-in-Publication Data
Names: Atwood, Megan, author.
Title: Palm reading / by Megan Atwood.
Description: North Mankato, Minnesota : Compass Point Books, 2019. | Series: The psychic arts | Includes bibliographical references and index.
Identifiers: LCCN 2018037317| ISBN 9780756561024 (hardcover) | ISBN 9780756561079 (ebook pdf)
Subjects: LCSH: Palmistry—Juvenile literature.
Classification: LCC BF921 .A885 2019 | DDC 133.6—dc23
LC record available at https://lccn.loc.gov/2018037317

Editorial Credits
Michelle Bisson, editor
Rachel Tesch, designer/illustrator
Svetlana Zhurkin, media researcher
Kathy McColley, production specialist

Photo Credits
Dreamstime: Loveliestdreams, 13, Roman Romanadze, 10 (top); Newscom: Design Pics, 11 (bottom), World History Archive, 10 (bottom right); Shutterstock: alexandre zveiger, 20, AMC Photography, 8, Anna Khomulo, 24, bodom, 10 (bottom left), Catalin Petolea, 23, Dmytro Zinkevych, 22, Dragon Images, 18, EQRoy, 10 (middle left), Everett Historical, 11 (top), In Green, 17, L.F, 10 (middle right), misspicha, 45 (bottom), Monkey Business Images, 19, newphotoservice, 6, paffy, 4, Prostock-studio, cover (front), rnl, 16, science photo, 25, Selenophile, 27, SiiKA Photo, cover (background), SpeedKingz, 26, ZinaidaSopina, 45 (top)

Printed and bound in the United States of America
PA49

TABLE OF CONTENTS

CHAPTER 1
Palms Up: An Introduction...5

CHAPTER 2
Palm Reading Through the Ages: The History
and Science of Palm Reading 9

CHAPTER 3
The Shape of Things: Palm Gazing 15

CHAPTER 4
Looking for Love: Talking about
the Heart and Head Lines 29

CHAPTER 5
Finding Your Destiny: Looking at
the Life and Fate Lines...37

CHAPTER 6
Make It Your Own!..43

    Palmistry Glossary 47

    Additional Resources 47

    Index 48

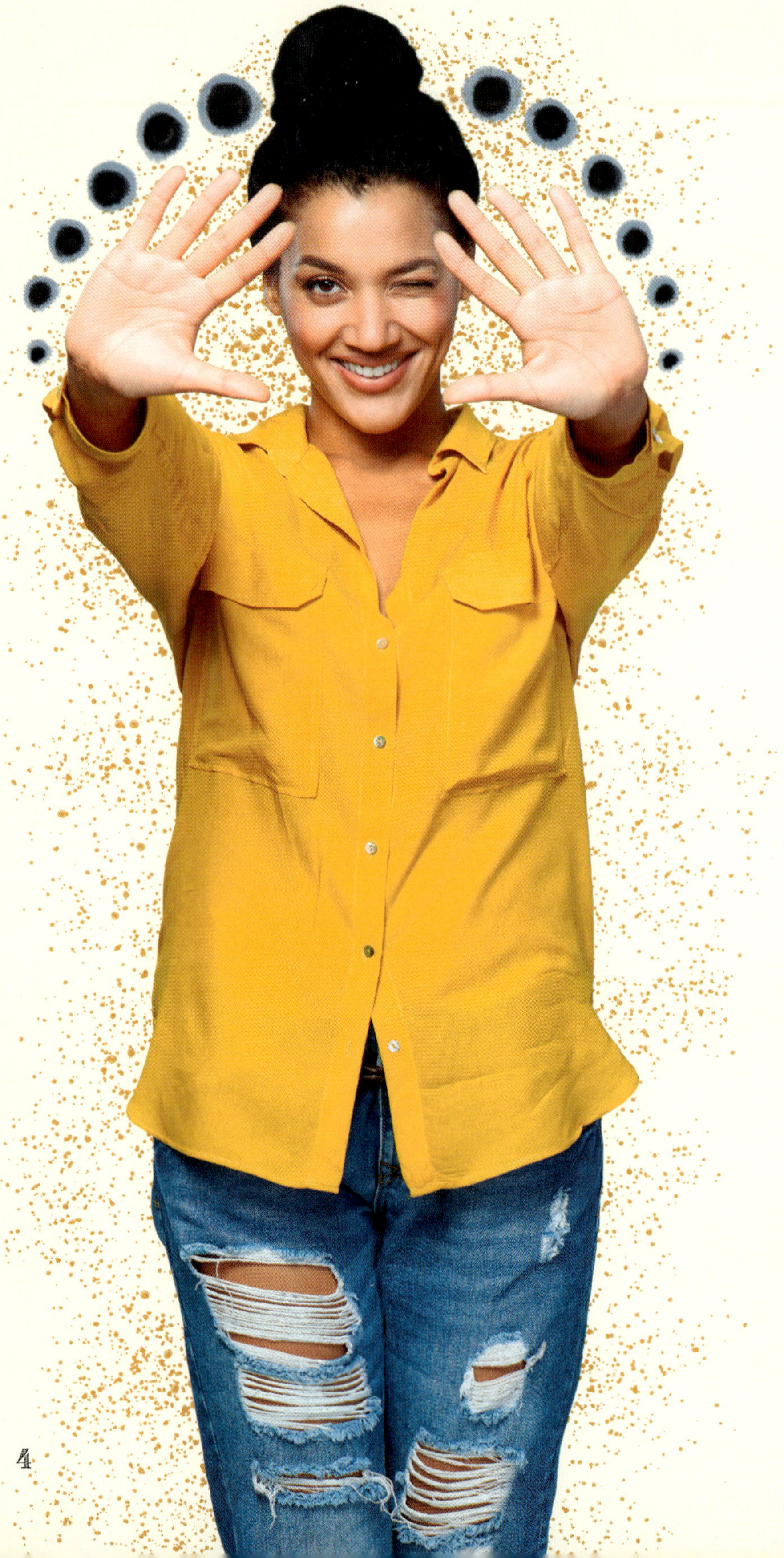

CHAPTER 1

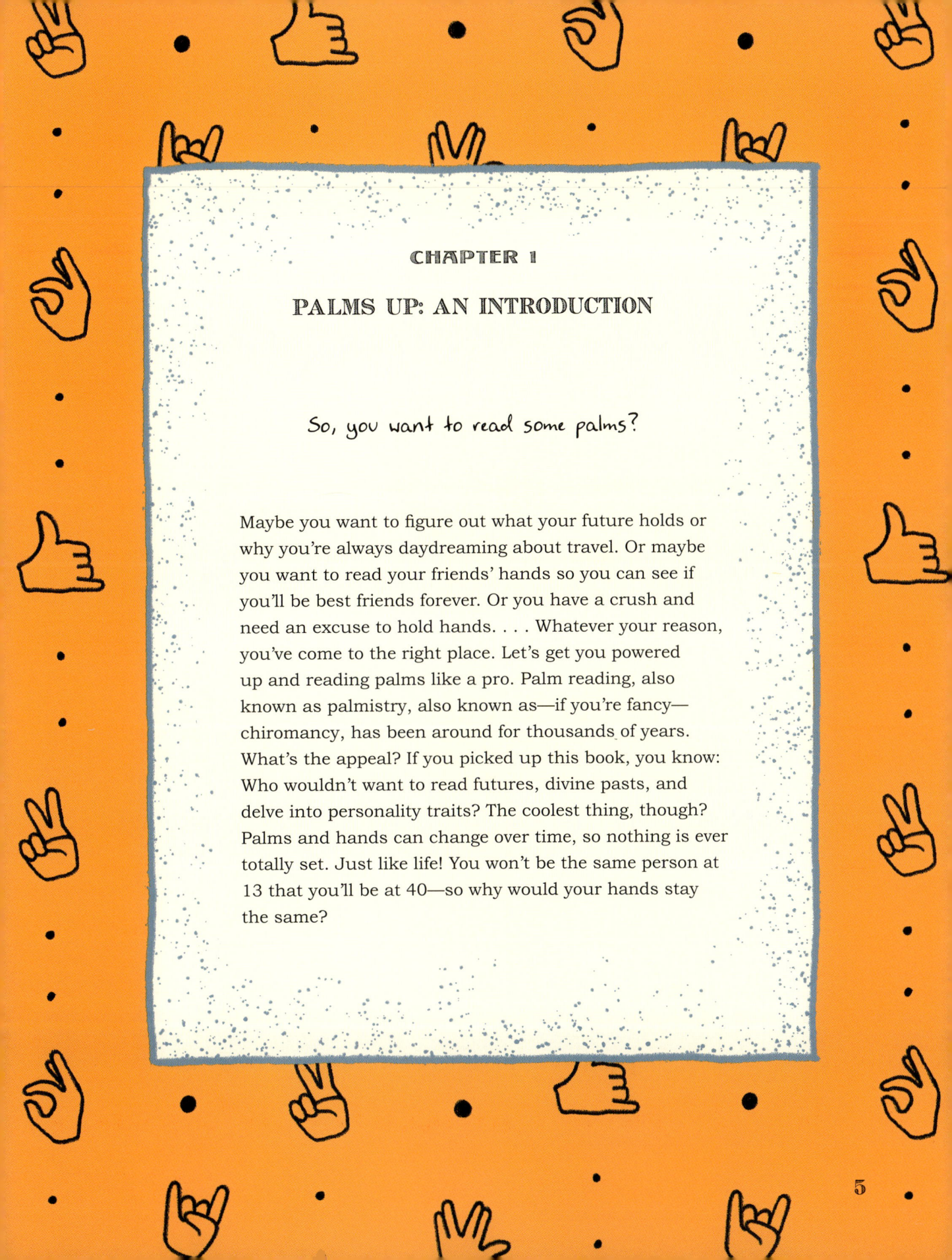

PALMS UP: AN INTRODUCTION

So, you want to read some palms?

Maybe you want to figure out what your future holds or why you're always daydreaming about travel. Or maybe you want to read your friends' hands so you can see if you'll be best friends forever. Or you have a crush and need an excuse to hold hands. . . . Whatever your reason, you've come to the right place. Let's get you powered up and reading palms like a pro. Palm reading, also known as palmistry, also known as—if you're fancy—chiromancy, has been around for thousands of years. What's the appeal? If you picked up this book, you know: Who wouldn't want to read futures, divine pasts, and delve into personality traits? The coolest thing, though? Palms and hands can change over time, so nothing is ever totally set. Just like life! You won't be the same person at 13 that you'll be at 40—so why would your hands stay the same?

YOUR BODY, YOUR FUTURE

PALMS AREN'T THE ONLY BODY PARTS READ THROUGH THE AGES. CHECK OUT THESE OTHER (SOMETIMES SUPERGROSS) WAYS PEOPLE HAVE TRIED TO TELL THE FUTURE USING THEIR OWN BODIES:

GASTROMANCY

Those sounds coming from your stomach? Well, your gut could literally be talking to you! See if you can hear your future between lunch and dinner. (Nowadays, gastromancy means crystal ball gazing—much more appetizing!)

MOLEOSOPHY

Some people think that moles are just a bunch of cells clustered together on your body. But those people have no imagination! Pay attention to the placement and patterns of your moles, and you just might see what your future holds.

OMPHALOMANCY

If anyone ever accuses you of belly-button gazing, tell them you're doing important work: You're predicting the future!

ONYCHOMANCY

Before you clip your fingernails, take a look at their shape, texture, color, and all sorts of things to figure out exactly who you are at your core.

PEDOMANCY

You know what else has lines besides palms? Your feet! Step right up to your future by reading the lines on the bottoms of your feet.

IT'S SOLE ENLIGHTENING!

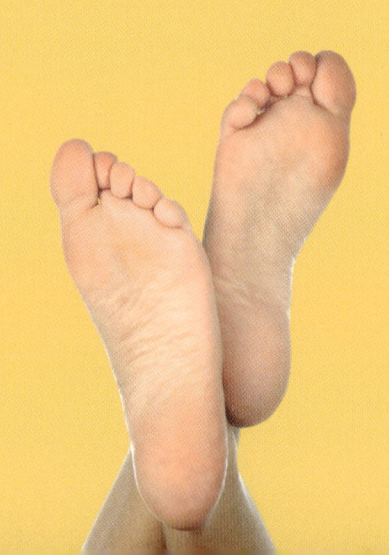

FIVE FRIENDLY RULES

Once you learn some techniques, you may be tempted to read *everyone's* hands all the time, even if they haven't asked you to. After all, you worked hard to get this power, right? So, why not use it?

1. First of all, it's ESSENTIAL that the person whose hand you're reading has asked you to do it. This is a new power you have—make sure not to abuse it!

2. Second, remember that this book is only an introduction to palm reading—there's a lot more to learn if you're really interested. Make sure to check out this book's additional resources to find out more.

3. Third, palm reading—and all the psychic arts, really—have a lot of gray areas. That is, people interpret things differently. If you read a line one way in a palm, someone else may see it in a different light. You want to make sure that if you're reading other people's hands, they understand that. And if you see something in a palm that seems really grim, remember: You are only getting glimpses of things. Never tell people they are going to die, or that a tragedy will befall them. You don't know for sure, and believing something bad is in their future could be devastating.

4. Fourth, remember that people who are asking you to read their palms may be looking to you for some wisdom. Treat them kindly and as you would want to be treated. Activate your empathy!

5. Last but not least, fifth, make sure not to share what you've read with others. The reading should stay between the two of you.

Now to the fun part:

THE ART OF PALM READING!

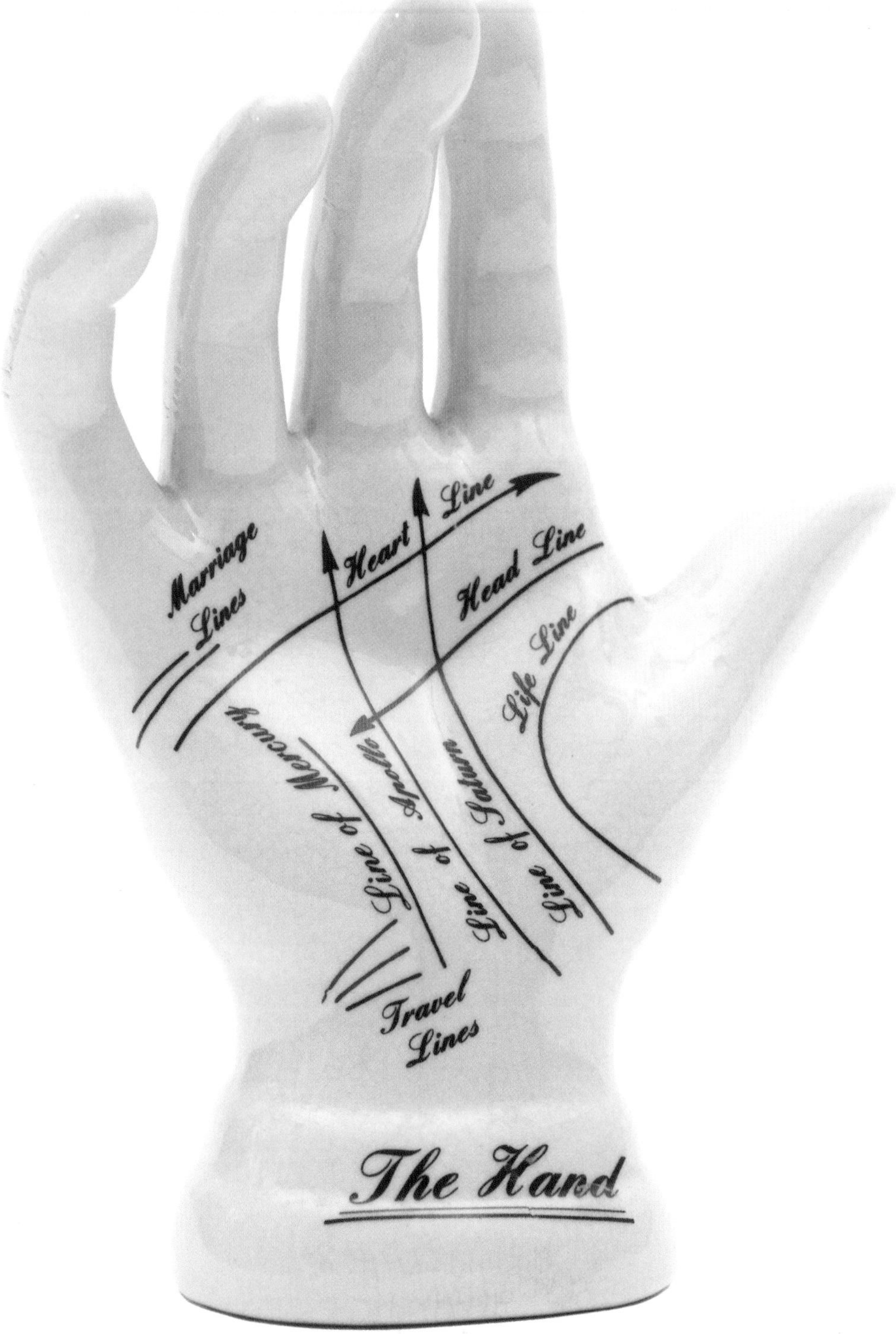

CHAPTER 2

PALM READING THROUGH THE AGES: THE HISTORY AND SCIENCE OF PALM READING

People have been obsessed with their own hands for centuries. Do you know there is a cave in Borneo, Spain, where ancient people made a bunch of handprints? This happened around 8,000 BC. That's a LONG time ago. So, who read the first hand?

Though there is no specific date for when the art of reading hands started, practitioners believe it may have begun in India with the Roma people more than 4,000 years ago. Some say that ancient Hindu holy scriptures, the Vedas, contain directions and references to reading palms.

Around the same time that ancient Indians and Roma started reading palms, Chinese medical texts began mentioning the importance of the lines on hands. Palmistry became an integral part of Chinese medicine. Chinese people understood the importance of hands in more than one way: According to a document about crime found in 3rd century BC China, the Chinese knew that fingerprinting could be used to solve crimes.

The Fortune Teller, painted by
Caravaggio in 1571

replica of prehistoric rock art
from the cave of Altamira

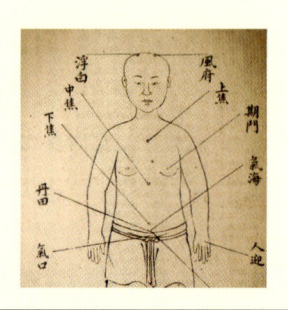

a page from an ancient
Chinese medical book

ancient book at Varanasi,
Uttar Pradesh, India

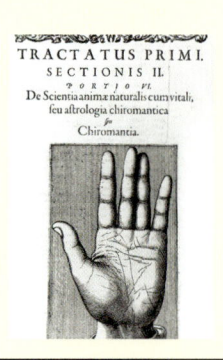

title page of chapter on chiromancy from
Robert Fludd book, showing lines of the hand

10

The art of palmistry spread to Europe soon after its appearance in Asia. Palm reading legend says palmistry played a big part in ancient Greece. Fragments of an essay from the philosopher Aristotle appear to be about palmistry, and some say he passed on his knowledge to his student, Alexander the Great, the future king of Greece. And then Alexander conquered tons of places and brought the art of palm reading with him.

ARISTOTLE PASSED ON HIS KNOWLEGE ABOUT PALMISTRY.

Palmistry continued to be a crowd pleaser for years, until, during the Middle Ages, the early Christian empire opposed palm reading and all other forms of divination. So for a few centuries, palmistry had fewer practitioners—but that didn't stop it. Palm reading managed to pass from culture to culture until it rose in popularity again.

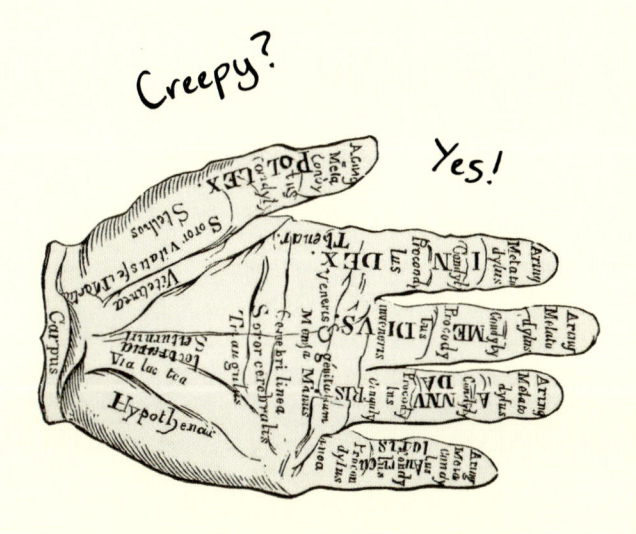

Aristotle

Alexander

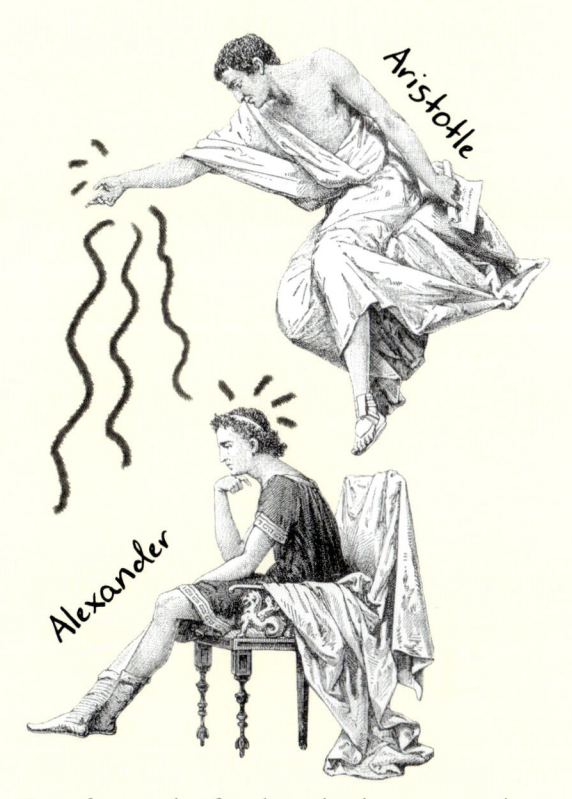

Fast-forward a few hundred years, and palmistry started to come out of the shadows in the West. The Victorian era (1847–1901) saw the hand hit its heyday in Europe and the United States. People believed that the hand could tell the character of the person it was attached to. In fact, during this time, many sculptures featured disembodied hands. Creepy? Yes! But still kind of cool.

And nowadays? Well, you're reading this book, right? *The Atlantic*, *The New York Times*, ThoughtCo, Bustle, HelloGiggles, and many more have published articles about palm reading in the past couple of years. Type "palm reading" into a search engine online and you could keep yourself busy for years! Or end up spending a lot of money on Internet palm readers. And, of course, there are many, many books on the subject.

Creepy? Yes!

But still kind of cool...

So wait a minute, you might be saying.

DOES THIS PALM READING THING ACTUALLY WORK?

That is a good question.

HOW COULD IT POSSIBLY?

And here is the definitive answer:

NOBODY KNOWS.

But here are a couple of interesting, science-related facts about hands for you to consider . . .

- Ridges on your hands are formed before you're born. Even identical twins don't have the same patterns on their hands.

- Take a look at your index finger and your ring finger. Either hand will do. If your ring finger is taller than your index finger, that means you were exposed to more of the hormone testosterone in the womb. So what does that mean? You might be better at endurance activities, but also might take more risks or be more aggressive.

- And who knows what else might come to light about hands and their human owners?

Does this mean that palmistry is 100 percent accurate?

No.

PALMISTRY IS AN ART, NOT A SCIENCE.

YOU are in charge of your own life.

The lines on your palm are only a part of you. And if you're reading for others, make sure they know that they are in control of their own lives too—not in the control of their hands.

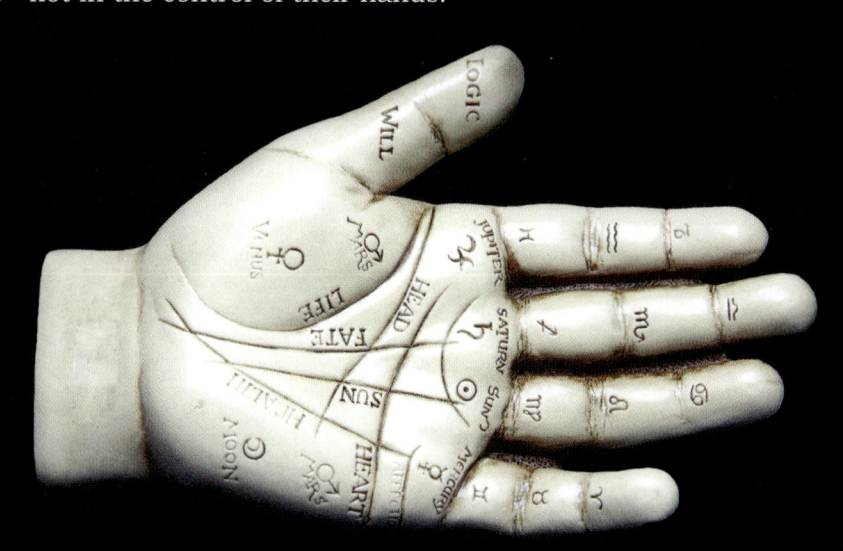

IT'S FUN TO SEE WHAT A PALM CAN TELL YOU, ISN'T IT?

EARTH

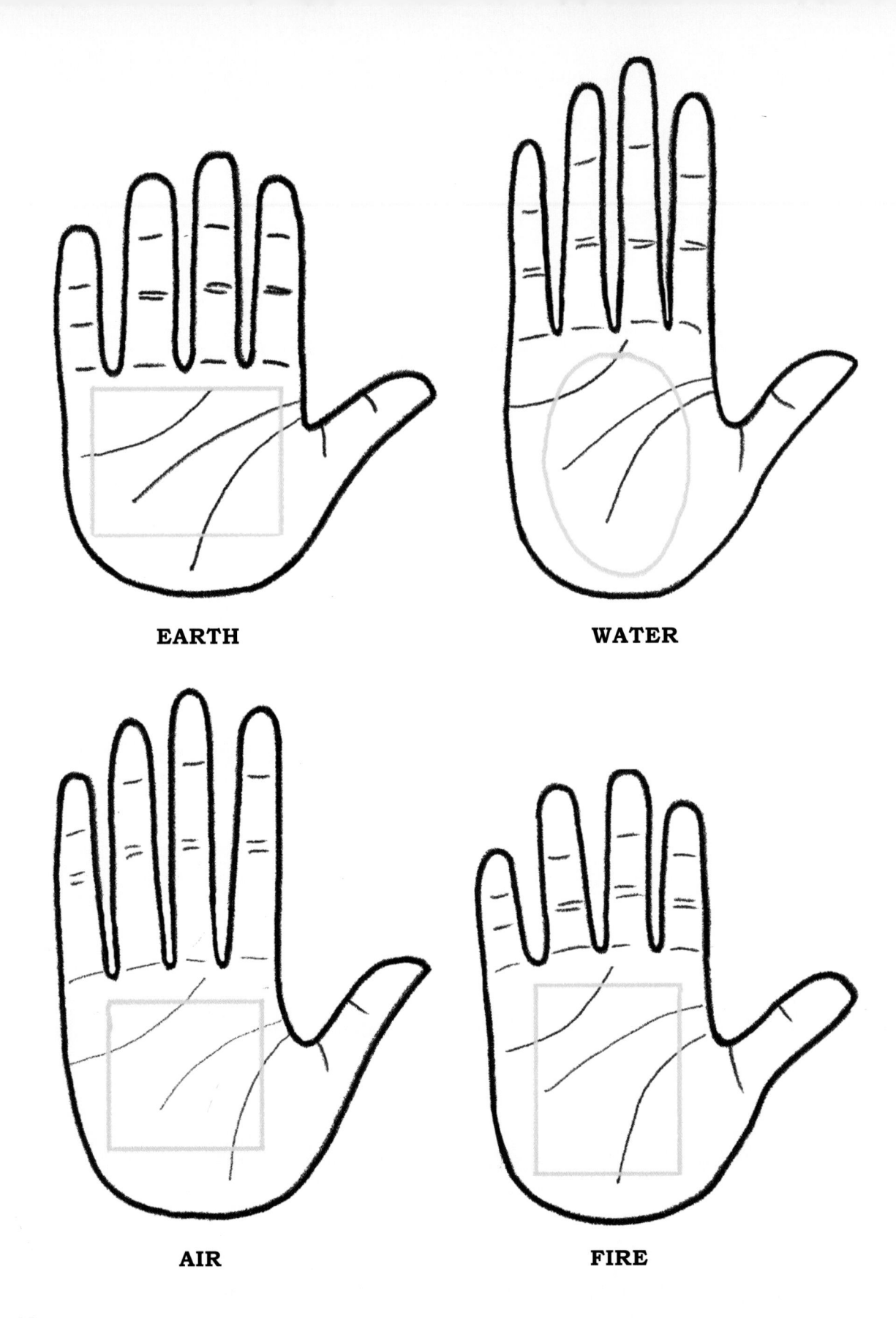

WATER

AIR

FIRE

CHAPTER 3

THE SHAPE OF THINGS: PALM GAZING

Before reading the lines of the hand, look at the shape. In palmistry, even the general shape of your palm has meaning. While there are many different types of palms, the four basic hand shapes correspond to the elements of earth, air, water, and fire. Check out these descriptions to see which one fits you!

AIR HAND

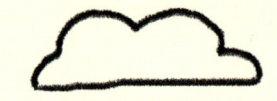

thinker

People with long, rectangular palms and long fingers with defined knuckles have air hands. The length of your palm is equal to the length of your fingers with this type of hand. If you have this type, you're a thinker! You like to talk things out and probably throw a bunch of theories around like confetti. You're a shoo-in for the debate team and you're probably a whiz at languages and technology. You may also be the person your friends come to for unbiased opinions or to discuss new ideas or fresh ways of thinking about things. Because you love to explore new places, travel will always be in your future. The downside? Well, you might stress out a bit much. Since you like thinking, chances are you like school and want it to reflect how smart you are. Which means you might be a bit of a perfectionist.

EARTH HAND

practical

Do you have wide, square-shaped palms with shortish fingers that are about the same height as your palms? You may have earth hands. With this type of hand, chances are you like nature and hiking, or other outdoor activities that keep you close to all that is natural. It also means you're probably even-keeled, honest, loyal, and peaceful. If your friends need some practical advice, they'll come to you. "Practical" is your middle name. You love classes where you get to DO things—you prefer experiences and movement over sitting around thinking about things. The downside? You might have trouble letting your imagination run free.

WATER HAND

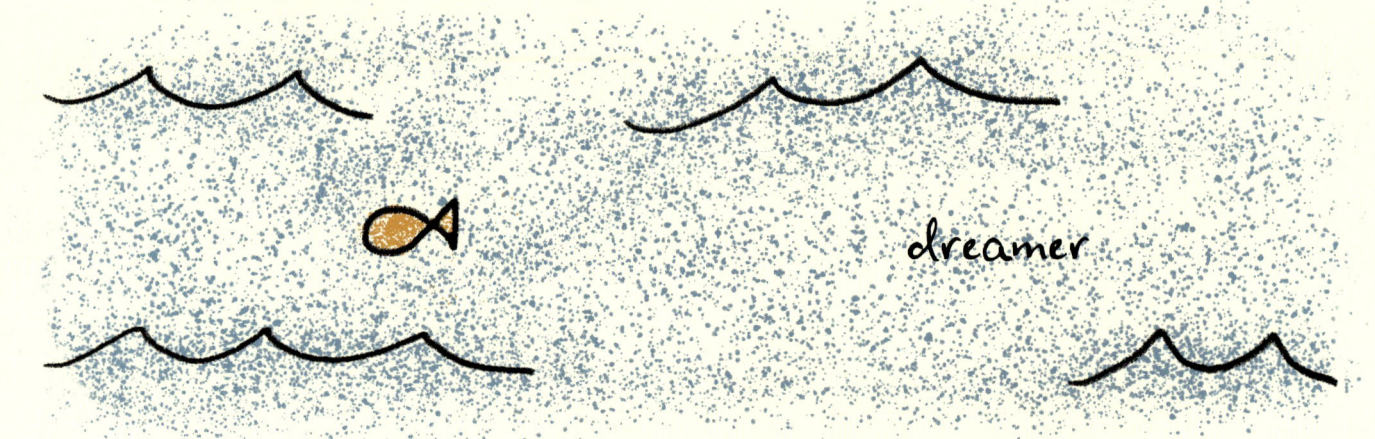

dreamer

If you have long, thin fingers and long palms, you probably have a water hand. Note: This does not mean a SWEATY hand. If you have a water hand, you're probably artistic and dreamy. At some point you may have been called too sensitive. Don't listen to that—you're a dreamer! Your imagination and artistic nature will produce some great things if you let them. Not to mention, you're superintuitive, so you can probably guess the mood your friend is in before he does. Your friends come to you when they need to be understood and accepted.

The downside? You might be a little less practical than others. Maybe some forgotten homework here or there, or possibly some daydreaming could get you in trouble. Find yourself an earth-hand friend so you can balance each other out!

18

FIRE HAND

go-getter

If your palm is rectangular, but taller than your fingers, you are probably a fire hand. Your hands might even be a little warm and flushed. Fire-hand people are go-getters: You like to lead, start new projects, and get things done. When you come into a room, everyone knows you're there. You have presence! People should get out of your way—you have things to do! Friends rely on you to make the plans and to get things going. You are superindependent and like to do things your own way—and people know you'll get things done. The downside? You're probably a little impatient. You're normally a few steps ahead of others and don't do well with indecision. Also, you can wear yourself out. A power nap or some downtime or meditation might be helpful.

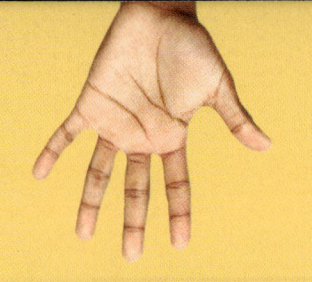

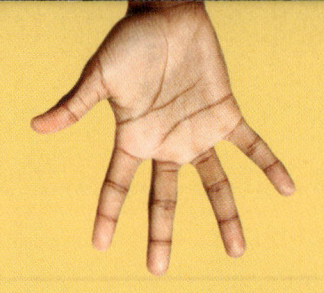

WHICH PALM?

TAKE A LOOK AT YOUR HANDS—CHANCES ARE, THEY HAVE DIFFERENT LINES AND DIFFERENT FOLDS, WHICH WOULD MAKE YOUR READINGS, WELL, DIFFERENT, DEPENDING UPON WHICH HAND YOU CHOOSE, RIGHT? SO WHICH ONE DO YOU READ?

There are a few schools of thought:

- Some palmists say the left hand is your potential, and the right hand is how you are living into that potential with your choices.

- Some say that you should read the left hand for girls and the right hand for boys.

- Some say you should choose your dominant hand to read.

For the purposes of this book, reading the hand you write with might be the simplest way to get to know all the lines. Or you could read both hands, compare the results, and go with the hand with the best results. After all, they're both your hands. Why not choose the interpretations that make the most sense to you?

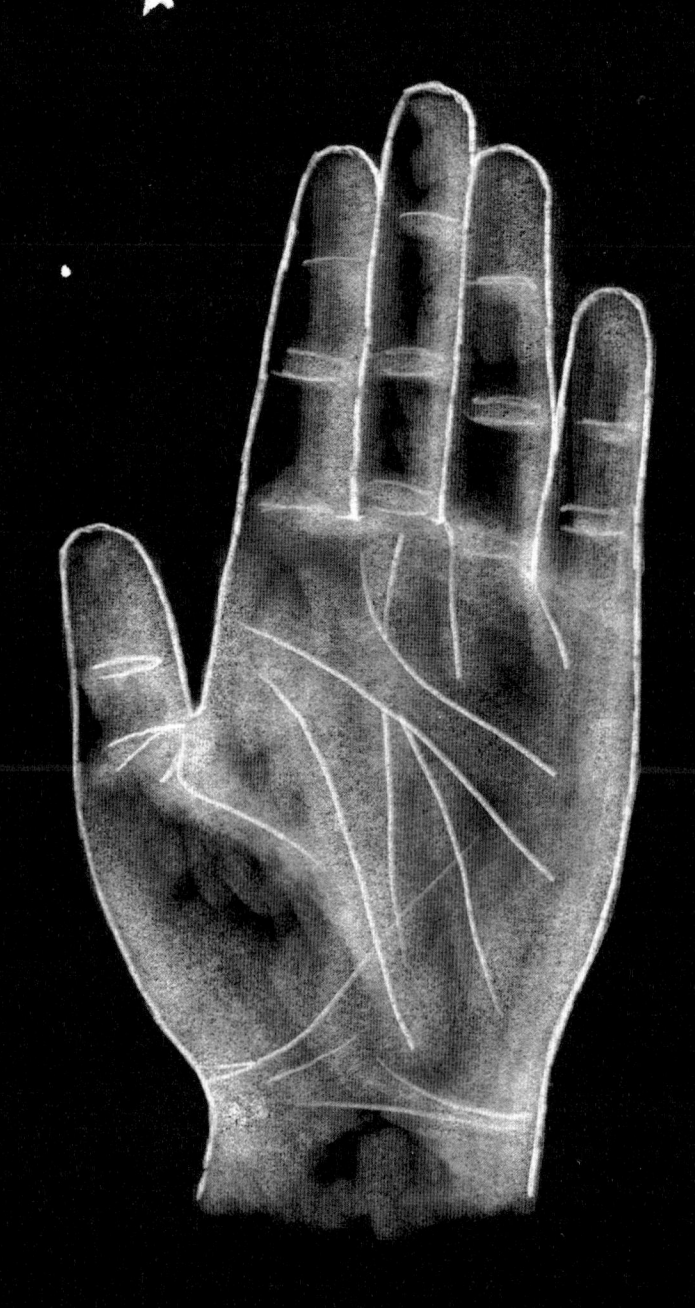

NOW THAT YOU'VE LOOKED AT THE GENERAL SHAPE OF YOUR HAND, TAKE A CLOSER LOOK AT YOUR PALM.

Not at the lines yet—that's in the next few chapters—but look at the fleshy bumps that form naturally on your hands. These pads are called mounts and are associated with different celestial bodies and their properties. The bigger the mount, the more influence it has over you. Here is where the mounts are located and what they mean:

JUPITER MOUNT

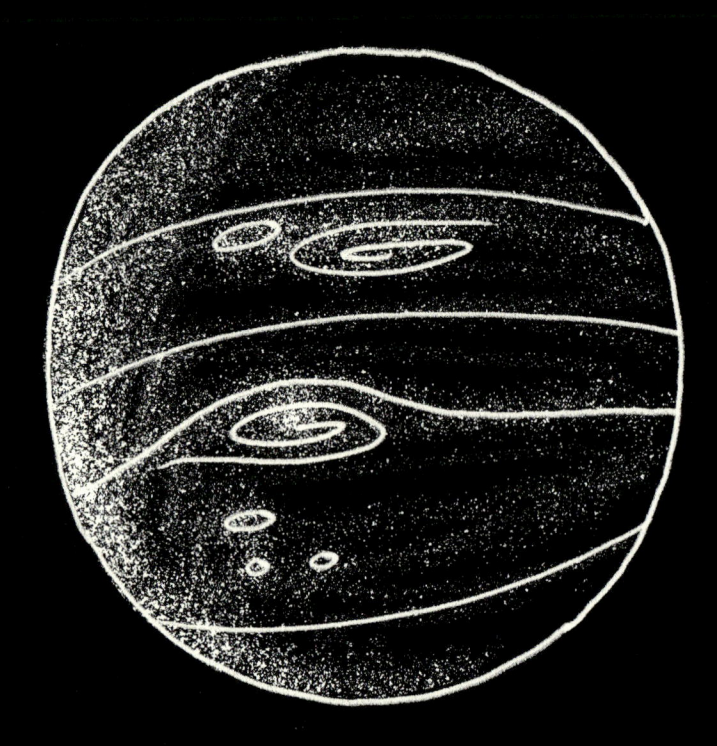

If this mount is well developed (that is, it's round and puffy), you have ambition and confidence, making you a good leader. You also care a lot about the world and everyone in it. You're not afraid to assert yourself to get what you need! Watch out, though—too much of a good thing could make you arrogant. So make sure to curb those tendencies if they're there and stick to being a great leader!

Under the Index Finger:

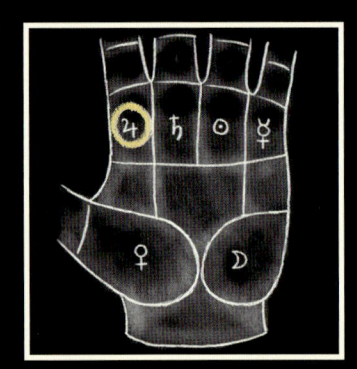

SATURN MOUNT

If this area is well developed on your palm, you're a hard worker, cautious, and have a lot of self-discipline. You're probably good at saving money and sacrificing for larger goals. But be careful—if you go too far, you might get depressed and a little too serious. Don't forget to have fun every once in a while!

Under the Middle Finger:

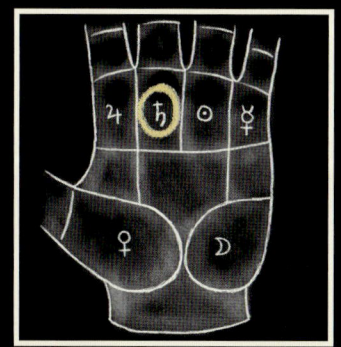

APOLLO, OR SUN, MOUNT

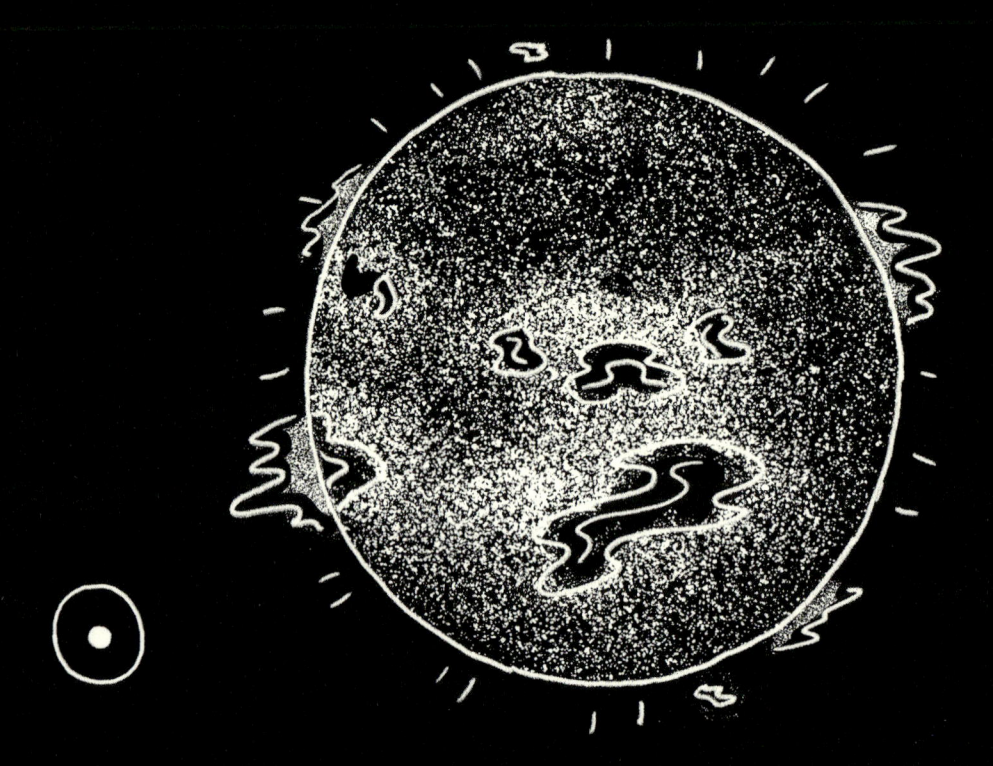

This mount has two pads under the ring finger. And if these mounts are well developed, you are probably super-charming. Does that sound like you? Are you the life of the party? The spontaneous road trip type of person? Lucky, talented, and happy? You can thank the Sun mount! If this mount is overdeveloped, though, watch out for a quick temper and easily changeable mood tendencies. Stick with your happy side!

Under the Ring Finger:

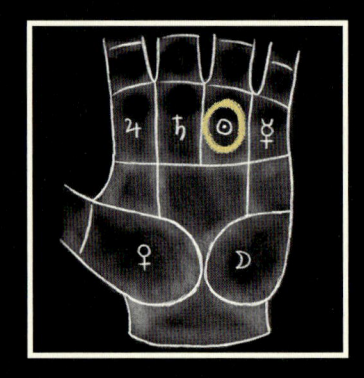

MERCURY MOUNT

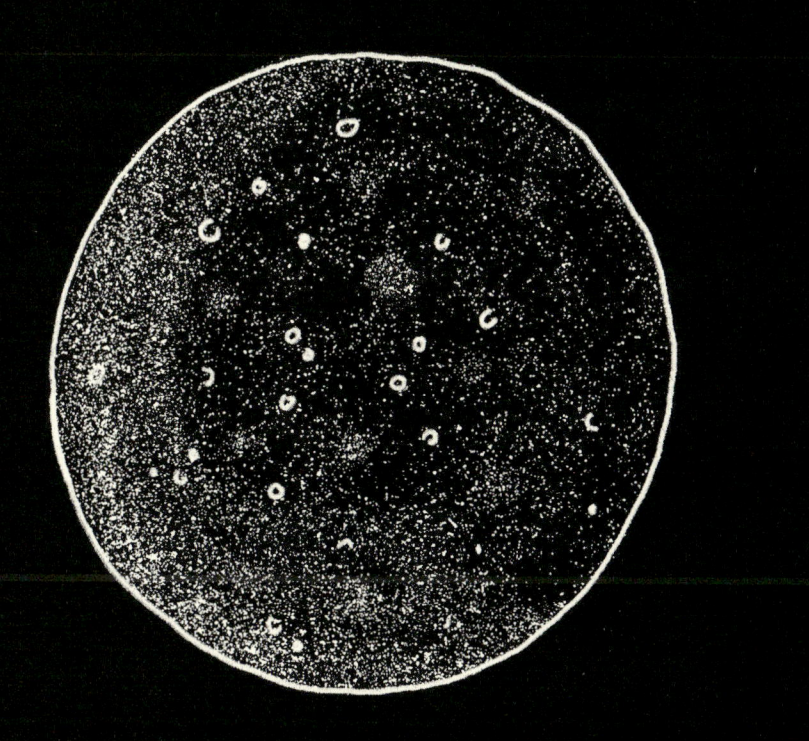

If this area is well developed on your palm, you love to talk, you love to solve problems, and you love to move. You're probably really into sports and you love school subjects that have concrete answers: Think STEM classes. A spreadsheet just might make you happy! If this area is too defined, you should be careful: You might get addicted to working. Look up from your homework every once in a while—there's lots more to life than just doing work!

Under the Pinky Finger:

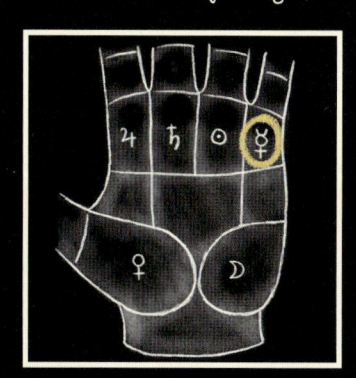

VENUS MOUNT

Venus is the planet of love and beauty. So take a look at the area below and around your thumb—if this area is nicely padded, you're a supercaring person and keeping things beautiful makes you happy. You're also empathetic and often think of others before yourself. Watch out: If this is too developed, you may have a problem saying "no" to helping others, so be sure to take care of yourself too!

Around Your Thumb:

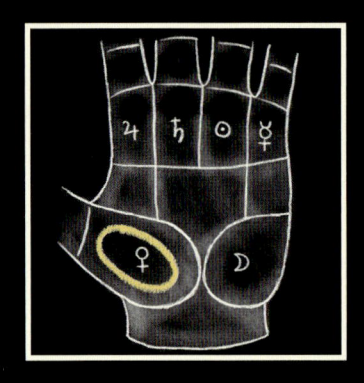

LUNA, OR THE MOON, MOUNT

If this area of your palm is nicely padded, you love the mystical, you're supersensitive, and you have awesome intuition. You probably love to spend time alone, dreaming and imagining a different world. Your friends probably call you psychic—and it's true, you most likely know things you have no business knowing! Be careful: You could get too caught up in your imagination or confuse reality with fantasy. Make sure your plans are grounded in the real world when you make them!

Across from the Venus Mount, Under the Mercury Mount:

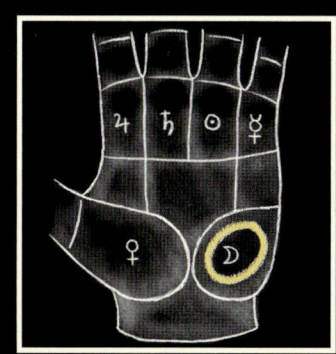

28

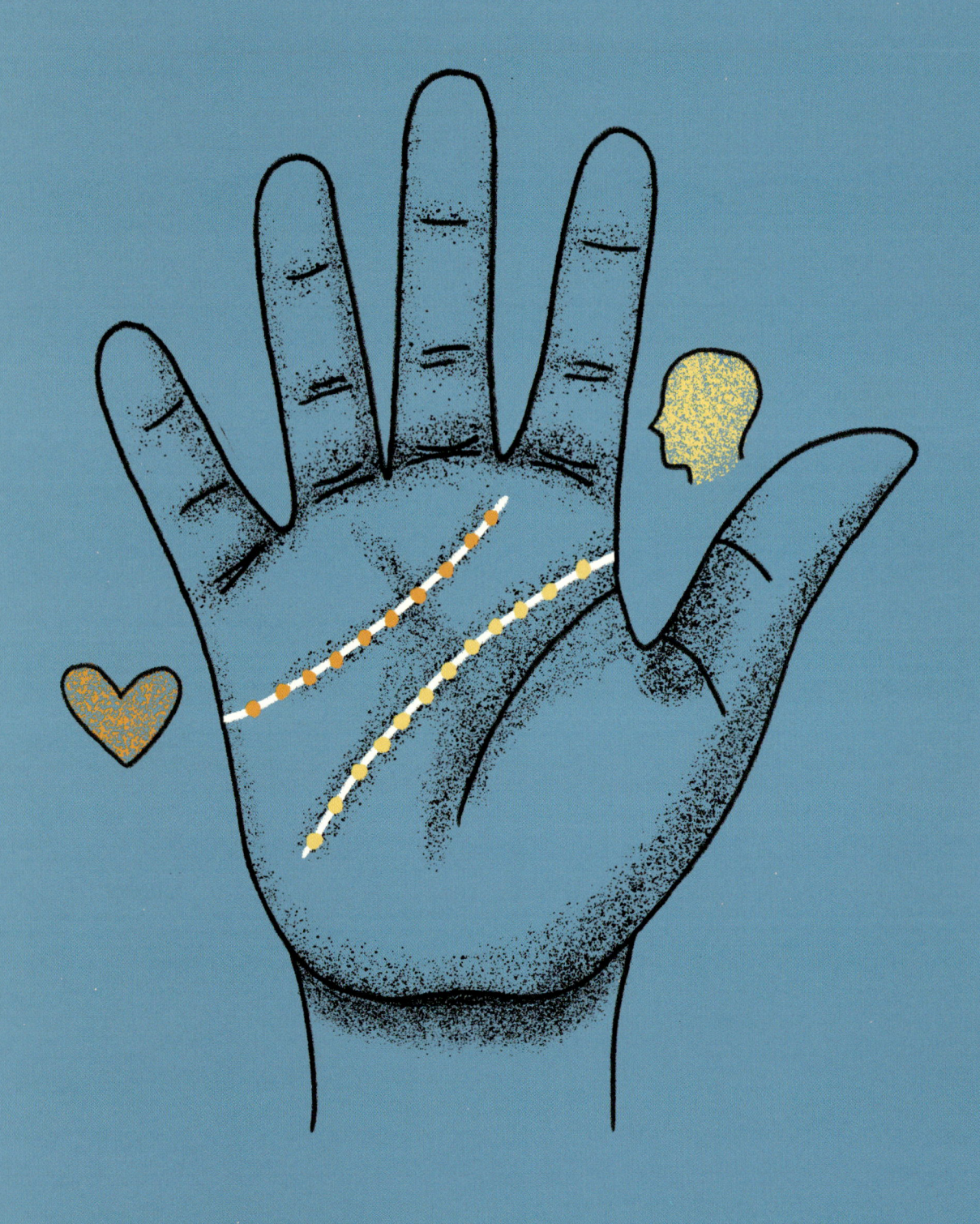

CHAPTER 4

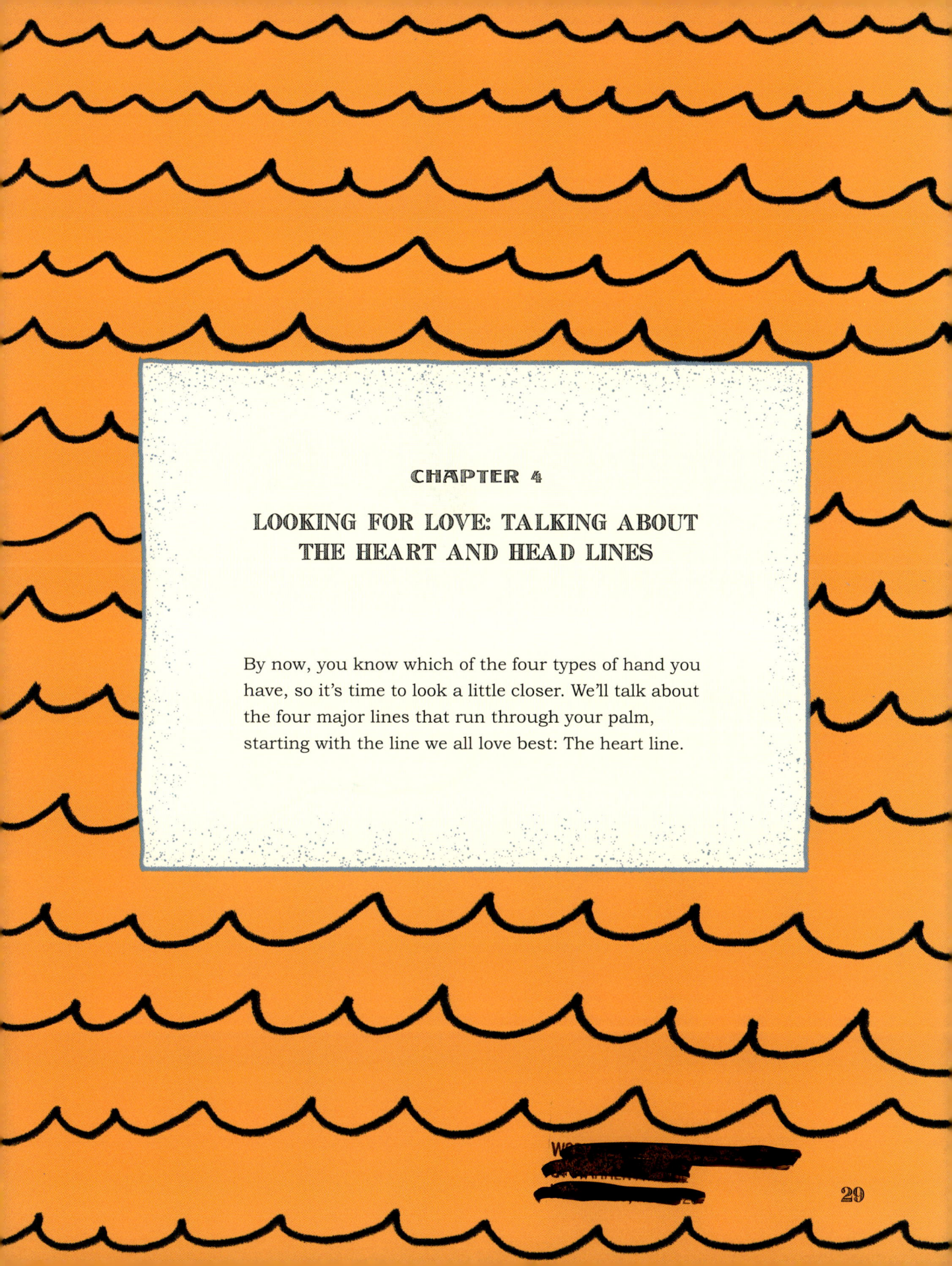

LOOKING FOR LOVE: TALKING ABOUT THE HEART AND HEAD LINES

By now, you know which of the four types of hand you have, so it's time to look a little closer. We'll talk about the four major lines that run through your palm, starting with the line we all love best: The heart line.

HEART LINE

Yes, this is the line of love!

This line deals with romantic love, but it also shows how you deal with emotions in general. The heart line is the first big line on your palm under your fingers, normally starting from someplace just under your fingers and traveling to the other side of your palm. The first thing to figure out is exactly where the line starts.

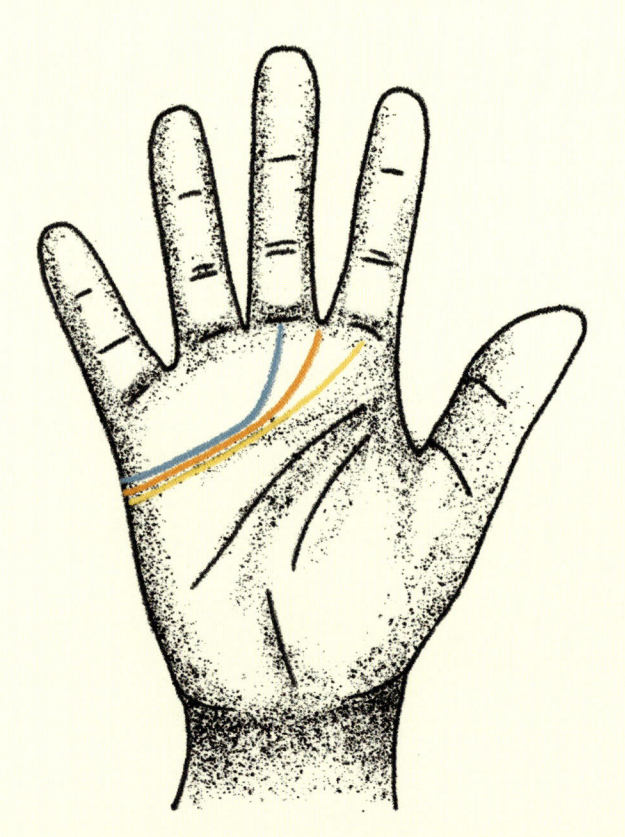

IF IT STARTS:

At the index finger: You have a lot of ambition and have a tendency to be a teensy bit selfish. But you make great decisions, and if you follow your heart, you'll be just fine.

Between the index finger and middle finger: You tend to give your heart away in love. You're also trustworthy and kind. You can make good decisions, but you have to think twice about things.

At the middle finger: You tend to be a bit of a loner and aren't super into relationships. That's totally fine—just make sure you keep other people's feelings in mind when interacting with them.

BELOW ARE A FEW OTHER THINGS TO LOOK FOR IN YOUR HEART LINE:

Short and straight: Freedom is important to you! You're not into clingy people.

Long and straight: You are rational and straightforward, but you think of other people before you make decisions.

Chainlike: You might give your heart away too easily and get hurt too quickly. Or, you will have deep, karmic relationships interconnected with other karmic things in your life.

Forked: You have a good balance between mental and emotional sides. Or, your relationships take a different path at a certain point in your life.

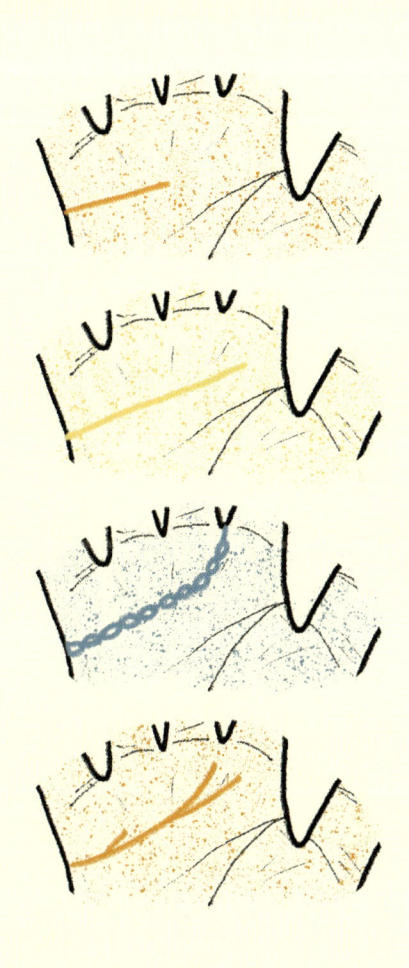

Digging a little deeper, we can look at the characteristics of the line and gain some insight. First, is your line curved or straight? If it's curved, you love *love*! You tend to think of others first and lean toward relationships over being a loner. If your line is straight, it suggests a no-nonsense approach to feelings and relationships. You may feel that you don't have time to deal with emotional entanglements so much.

Also, how deep is your line? If it's deep, that means you probably have a lot of friends and might be really serious with any potential significant others. If it's shallow, maybe relationships aren't the main focus of your life.

PRO TIP

WITH PALMISTRY, THERE IS SO MUCH TO REMEMBER. LOOKING FOR THE FOLLOWING TYPES OF LINES AND WHAT THEY GENERALLY MEAN WILL HELP YOU REMEMBER MORE. IF THE LINES YOU'RE LOOKING AT HAVE THESE CHARACTERISTICS, YOU CAN SEE WHAT THEY MEAN HERE:

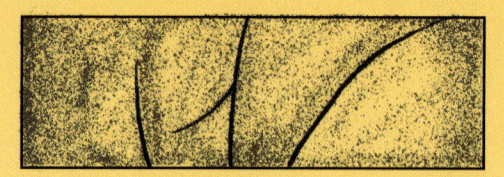

Deep lines mean the influence is really strong

Stars mean an intense occurrence, either good or bad, will happen

Shallow lines mean the influence is less intense

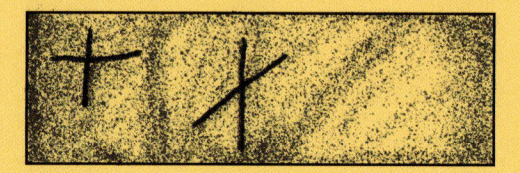

Crosses are significant incidents

Forked lines indicate a split or the decision to take a different path

Squares mean protection and blessing

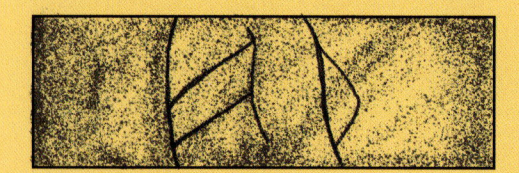

Islands are an interruption or change in direction to a path that will last a while

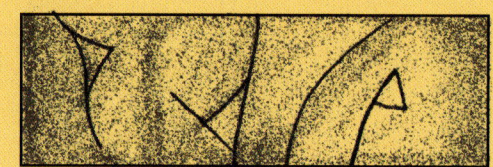

Triangles add brilliance to any line

HEAD LINE

Following your heart is great, but you should take your head along too!

The head line in palmistry shows how you use your intelligence, how you go about thinking, and how well you can concentrate and focus. Like the heart line, the head line can change throughout life—you can check it at different ages to see if you're living up to your potential.

The head line is below the heart line and starts somewhere between your index finger and your thumb.

⭐ *If your head line meets your life line between your thumb and index finger,* you might undervalue your capabilities and struggle with confidence.

⭐ *If your head line slopes downward,* you are sensitive and creative, and are probably superintuitive.

⭐ *If it meets up with your heart line,* you make decisions that take into account your feelings and the people around you.

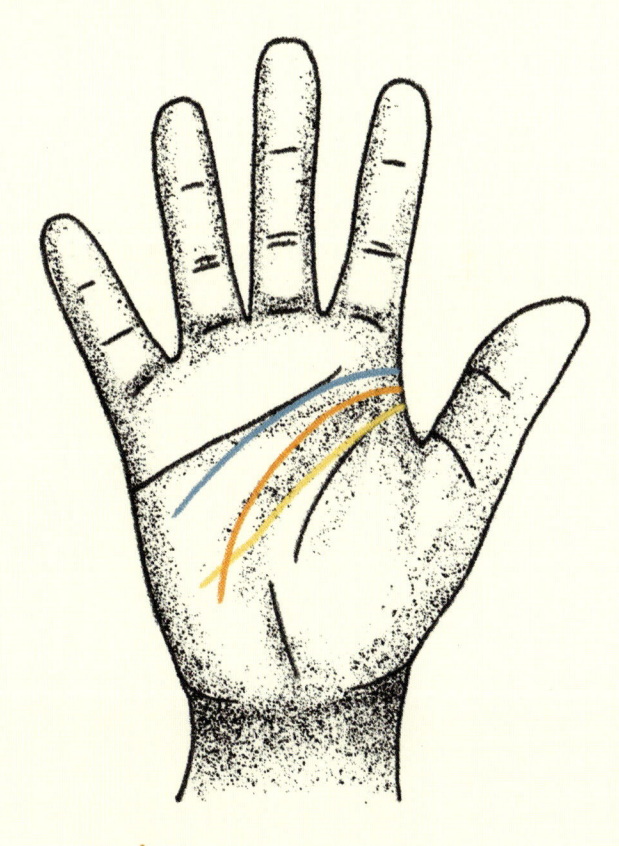

⭐⭐⭐ = head line variations

LET'S GO OVER SOME OF THE OTHER THINGS TO LOOK AT.

A deep line: You're able to focus on the task at hand and you love any pursuits of the mind! Your friends definitely want you for a study buddy.

A shallow line: Maybe you have some trouble concentrating? Or maybe you just think there are better things to do than thinking.

Curved: You're flexible in your thinking and are incredibly imaginative. You love digging underneath conversations for anything that's left unsaid.

Straight: You are practical and rational and are all about keeping it real.

LOOK FOR THESE THINGS IN YOUR HEAD LINE AS WELL:

Uneven or broken up: You'll have some changes in the way you think throughout your life.

Head line separated from life line: You are optimistic and independent, and you're probably an adventure-seeker.

Forked: If the end of your head line forks, this means you're great at seeing different sides of an argument. This is also sometimes called a "writer's fork" or a "lawyer's fork"—it means you're great with words! You'd also be a spectacular investigator or detective.

Trident (three lines forking from the end of your head line): You're brilliant! You might just be a genius, and your mind is versatile and open.

Crosses or X's: You might have to make some big decisions here and there throughout your life and may come up against some challenges. But sometimes these challenges bring you great success, and they help you think outside the box!

And there you have it!

You now know what you're looking for in both your heart and your head. Or at least what your PALM says you're looking for. Now that you know your tendencies, you can use this information to help you move forward.

How cool is that?

34

WHEN YOU SEE SOMETHING SCARY IN A HAND

LET'S SAY YOU ARE READING YOUR BFF'S HAND AND . . . UH-OH. SHE HAS ISLANDS AND CROSSES AND ABOUT EIGHT OTHER THINGS THAT LOOK LIKE CHALLENGES. IN FACT, IF YOU'RE READING HER PALM CORRECTLY, SHE'S GOING TO HAVE A MAJOR HEALTH SCARE SOMETIME IN HER LIFE. YOU DOUBLE CHECK IN THIS BOOK, YOU READ SOME WEBSITES, YOU CONSULT OTHER BOOKS, BUT ALAS, HER FATE SEEMS SEALED. WHAT DO YOU SAY?

Sorry, dude, you're going to have a hard life. Good luck!

I'm just the reader—it's not my job to fix your life for you.

Have you thought of being someone else?

The answer is: None of the above. The psychic arts are meant to help improve life, not make it worse or scare anyone. Plus, people have the power to change their lives. You're definitely going to want to introduce anything that isn't positive with the reminder that your friend can change anything in her life—these lines are written on a palm and not in stone. Look for ways to discuss difficult findings in a way that helps. Instead of "This cross on your fate line means you'll fail!" consider saying, "The cross might mean a challenge, but that will help you think outside the box!" If you're not sure how to talk about it, then don't bring it up. Always practice kindness and empathy and use good judgment.

36

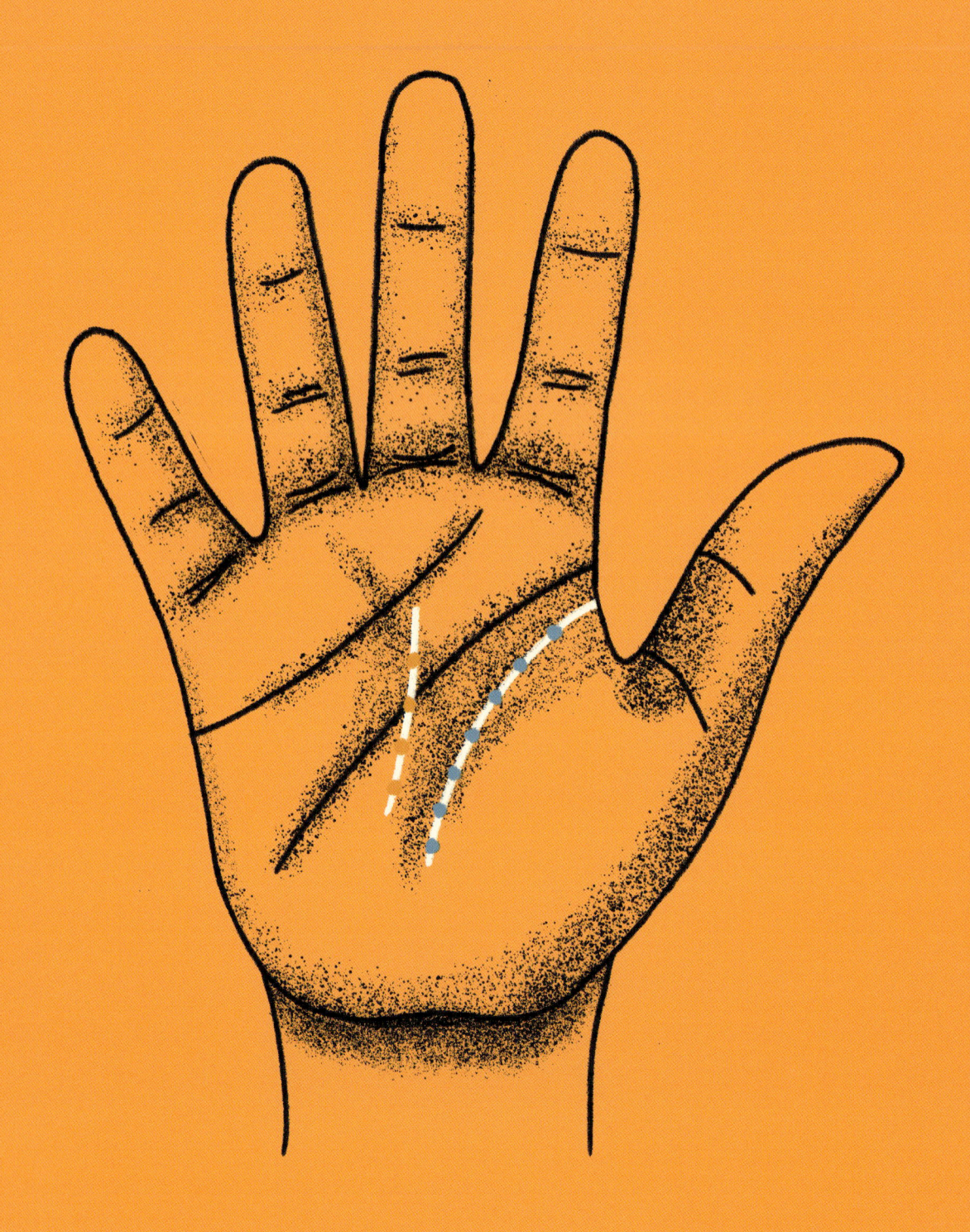

CHAPTER 5

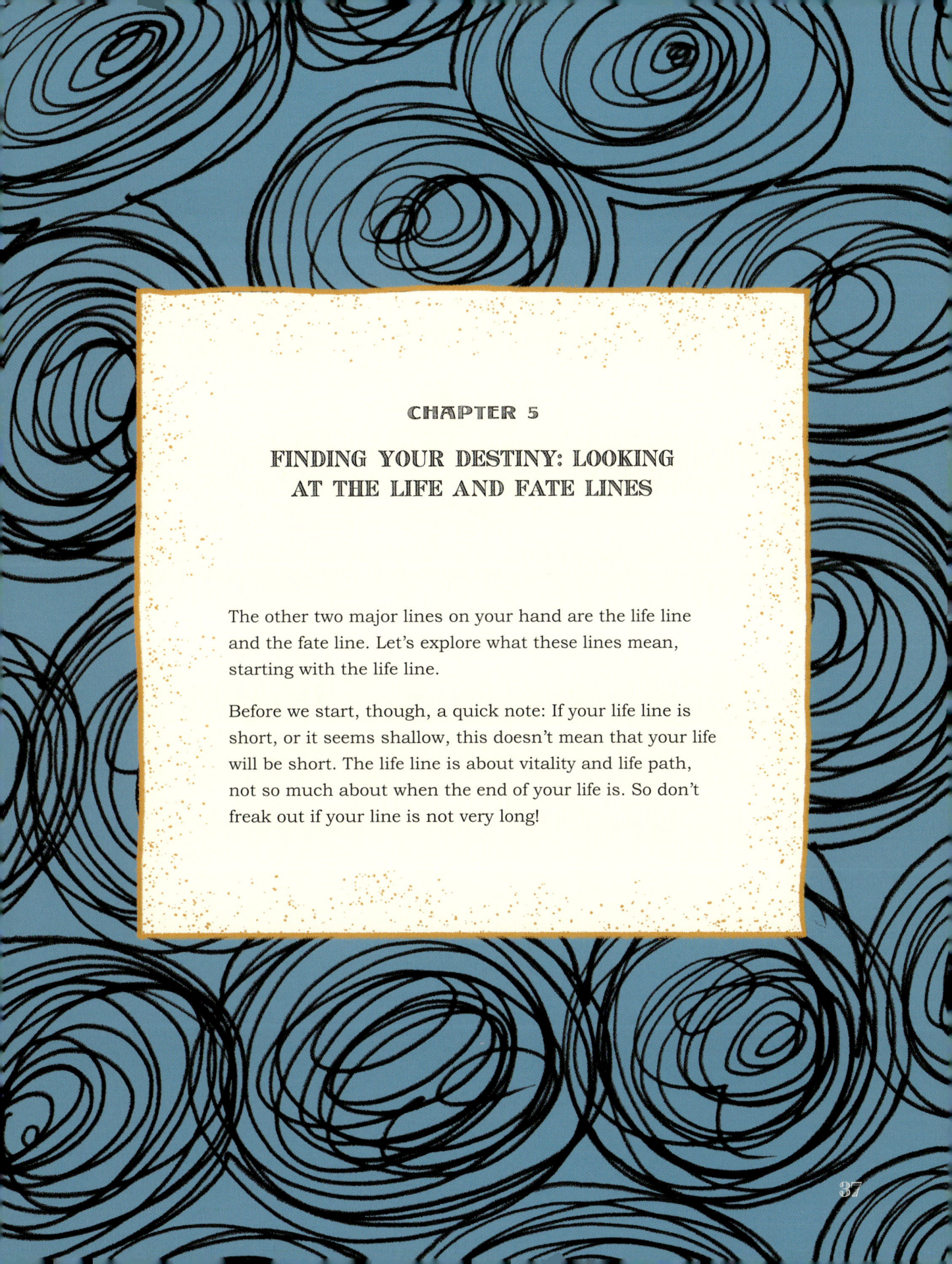

FINDING YOUR DESTINY: LOOKING AT THE LIFE AND FATE LINES

The other two major lines on your hand are the life line and the fate line. Let's explore what these lines mean, starting with the life line.

Before we start, though, a quick note: If your life line is short, or it seems shallow, this doesn't mean that your life will be short. The life line is about vitality and life path, not so much about when the end of your life is. So don't freak out if your line is not very long!

LIFE LINE

The life line starts in the same area as your head line: between the thumb and index finger. The life line wraps around your thumb and the mount of Venus and usually ends somewhere around the bottom of your palm. If you don't have a life line, don't worry—you're alive! Palmists believe that the absence of a life line means you might be a little extra anxious about things.

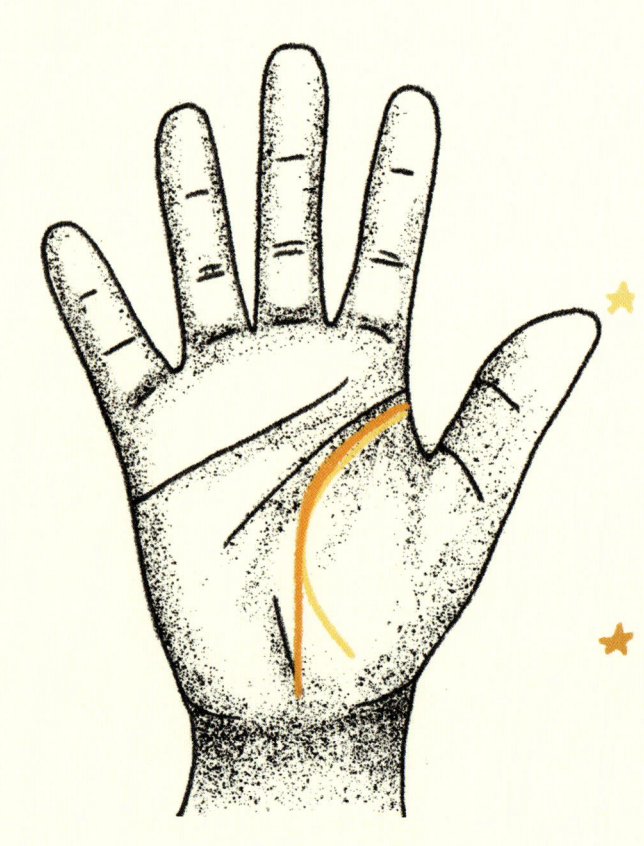

FIRST TAKE A LOOK AT HOW YOUR LIFE LINE CURVES.

⭐ *If it curves out and wide,* this means you are a magnetic, sympathetic, people person. Friends might invite you out to smooth things over in a social situation! If the line is straightish and closer to the thumb, with a narrow arc, you're probably a bit introverted. It takes you a while to warm up to people and for you to let them in.

⭐ *However, if your line is deep,* no matter where it is, you probably have a lot of energy and a zest for life. You might be a little intense, too, and try to live life to its fullest.

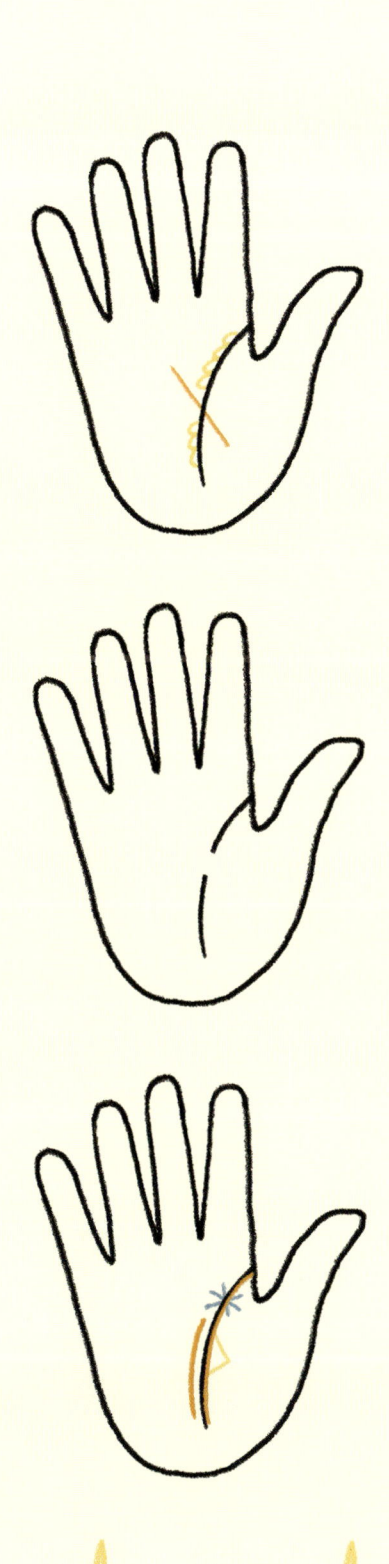

SOME OTHER THINGS TO LOOK FOR ON YOUR LIFE LINE:

Shallow: You might need a lot of naps! A shallow line says your energy may wane easily and you have to work hard to get yourself going.

Chained: You may have some illnesses here and there. Or your life will have a few shakeups now and then!

Crossbar: This is a horizontal line that may interrupt the life line occasionally. This could mean there'll be an important moment in a person's life where things may change.

Break in the line: If your life line breaks, but overlaps, this means you will have an interruption of some sort but come out well on the other side! If the line that continues on starts on the outside of the first line, you'll come out even stronger.

Star: This could be an explosive moment in your life, good or bad. You may even discover something huge!

Triangle: You have some brilliance happening in your life, and your energy is supported by your wisdom.

Double line: You just might have a soul mate! You'll have a partner to walk through life with.

FATE LINE

Now on to the fate line. This line is also called the destiny line or the Saturn line—the latter because the line is normally situated below the Saturn mount. Not everyone has a fate line, so if you don't see one, it's not because you don't have a fate! If you do have the line, it normally starts at the bottom of your palm (or in the middle of it), and runs straight up toward your middle finger, though it doesn't always go all the way up.

The fate line is similar to the life line in that it shows the path your life will take or the path your life has taken. But it can also show how secure you feel in your life, whether you feel you have a purpose in life, or the reactions you have to what has happened in your life.

★ If you believe in destiny, a deep fate line means you have a strong one—or it could mean you have a deep sense of purpose in your life.

★ If it runs all the way up your palm, you have a pretty strong destiny to follow. People who are movie stars or astronauts most likely have those lines.

★ And if the start of your fate line is joined to your life line, you make your own way in life. You know how to make decisions and move forward according to your own values, and you already know what you want to be.

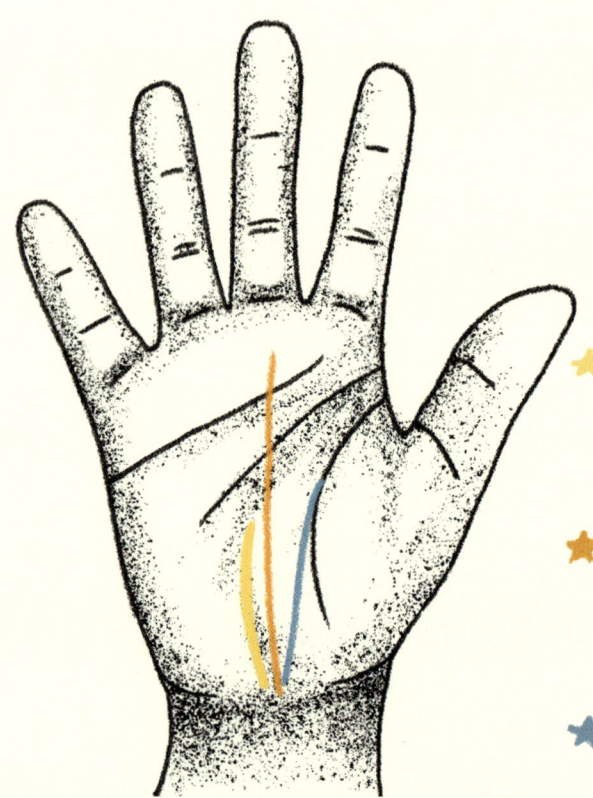

Some believe the fate line is about security in life—specifically, financial security.

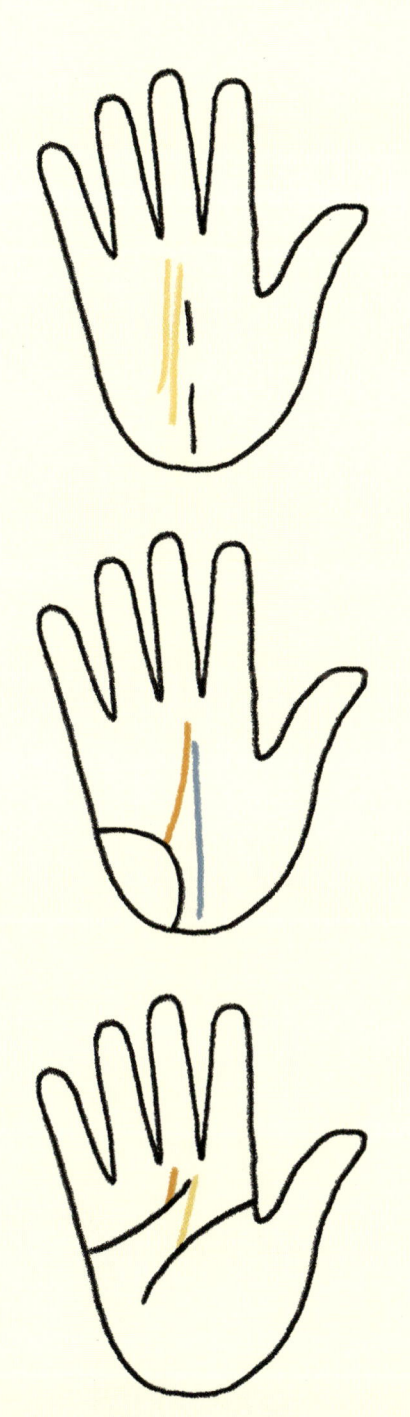

THERE ARE A LOT OF WAYS TO READ THIS LINE, BUT HERE ARE SOME THINGS TO LOOK FOR:

Deep: Another interpretation of a deep line could mean an inheritance.

Broken: If your fate line is broken near your head line, that means you'll change careers successfully. If there are a lot of broken places, you might have some stops and starts in your life.

Two lines: You're going to be really successful! Especially if both your lines are long. Maybe you could even have a successful partner who travels along with you.

Starts on the Luna mount: You'll be given a lot of help through life, most likely financial help.

Starts at the base of the palm: You're going to be famous! Start working on your head shots . . .

Begins at the head line: You'll be successful, but probably after 35 or so.

Begins at the heart line: You'll be successful later in life, probably after age 50. This is still good news!

Now you have read all about the four most important lines in palmistry—supercool, right? Next we'll talk about some of the minor lines to look for in a palm once you've mastered the major lines.

MINOR LINES

Not everyone has these minor lines. If you don't have some or all of these, it doesn't mean you don't have these qualities. But if you do, they can give you a bit more insight into your possibilities.

- **Creative line/success line. Also called the "Apollo line":** If you have a line that starts under your ring finger, you are probably really creative and will be successful using that creativity. This line can also mean fame, fortune, and success in all you do! The longer it is, the more this trait holds.

- **Guardian Angel line:** This line is on the inside of your life line and is very rare. If you have this line, some palmists believe you get a little help from your celestial friends—angels, that is. This could be a loved one who passed away or just a guardian angel, however you define it. This is a superlucky line to have! This line says you'll be helped through your whole life and have some good luck.

- **"Bracelets":** You know those lines right under your palm on your wrist? Those are called bracelet lines. If you have four of them, consider yourself lucky—you might live to be 100 or more!

- **Simian line:** Maybe reading this book and learning about the head line and the heart line seemed confusing to you. Perhaps you have one straight line across your palm. If that's the case, you have a simian line. But watch out—this could mean you're pretty stubborn. However, it could also just mean your head and your heart are perfectly aligned, making sure you'll be successful in life.

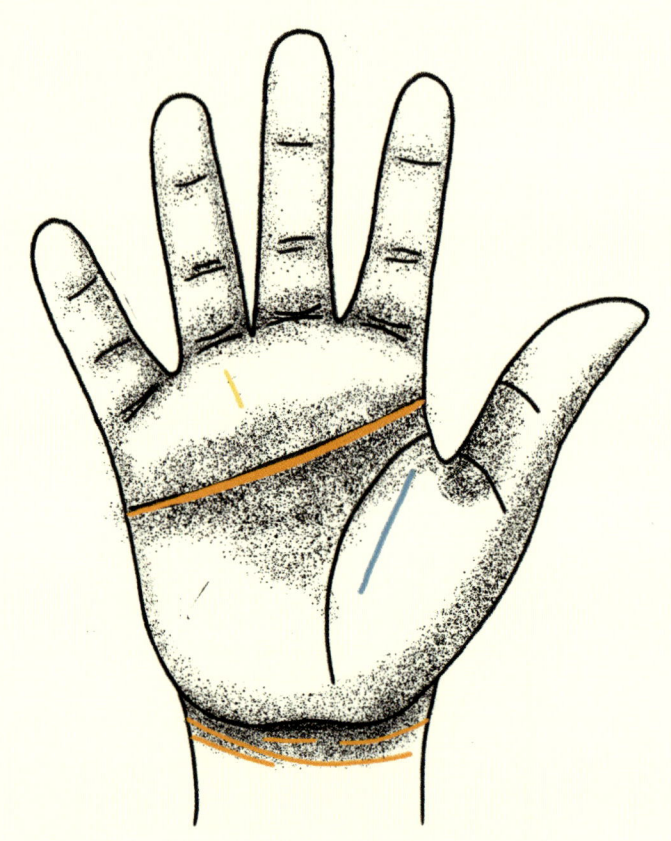

42

CHAPTER 6

MAKE IT YOUR OWN!

You've read through this book, and now you have the world in the palm of your hand! Or at least a start. If you decide you want to read your friends' hands, you can start with your close friends and move on from there as you get more comfortable.

Remember to let them know you're just starting out! It may seem overwhelming—there's a lot of information, and so many ways to read palms!

FOLLOW THESE STEPS TO BEGIN UNTIL YOU GET MORE AND MORE COMFORTABLE AND SKILLED AT IT.

1 Look at the shape of the palm and the fingers. Is it an earth hand? A fire hand? Are the fingers long and thin? Short and stubby? Is the hand dry?

2 Next look at the mounts. Are they rounded? Flat? Are some more pronounced than others?

3 Now's the time to look at the lines. You can start from the top of the hand on down, so you remember them all. Start with the heart line, go to the head line, then the life line, and, finally, the fate line if it's there.

4 Look to see if the line you're reading is deep or shallow, broken or whole, straight or curved.

5 In these lines, look for patterns—are there chains? Triangles? Stars or crosses? These will help you find what is unique about the person's palm you're reading.

Most importantly: Follow your intuition and speak with kindness! Chances are you are full of empathy, so engage that all through the reading.

PARTY!

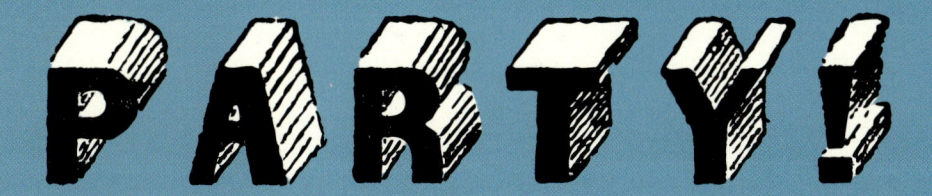

All right, fellow palm reader, it's time to put your skills to the test and most importantly, have some fun with it! Why not throw a palmistry-themed party? Some ideas for your awesome shindig:

FOOD

Of course, you're going to want to serve finger food, right? Think appetizers you can pick up with your fingers. And even food shaped like fingers. Try cooking a pizza, cutting it into strips, then cutting out triangles of a vegetable (like a pepper) and putting on a "fingernail." Or putting almond pieces on the end of a carrot stick. To complete your hand theme, make a spreadable salad, like tuna, to put on crackers topped with hearts of palm.

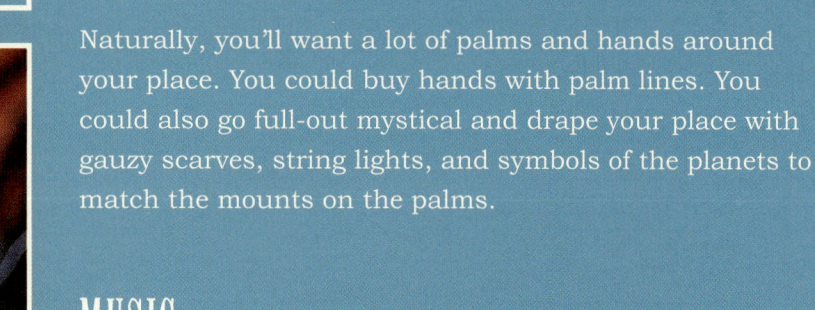

DECORATIONS

Naturally, you'll want a lot of palms and hands around your place. You could buy hands with palm lines. You could also go full-out mystical and drape your place with gauzy scarves, string lights, and symbols of the planets to match the mounts on the palms.

MUSIC

You'll want to play music your friends can get behind, of course. But why not throw in some songs that have "hand" in the lyrics? Some suggestions: "I Want to Hold Your Hand" by the Beatles; "Secondhand News" by Fleetwood Mac; "Hands of the Priestess" by Steve Hackett; and "He's Got the Whole World in His Hands" by Nina Simone.

Reading people's palms is a great responsibility and a lot of fun. Use your newfound power wisely and give me a high-five. You are officially a palm reader!

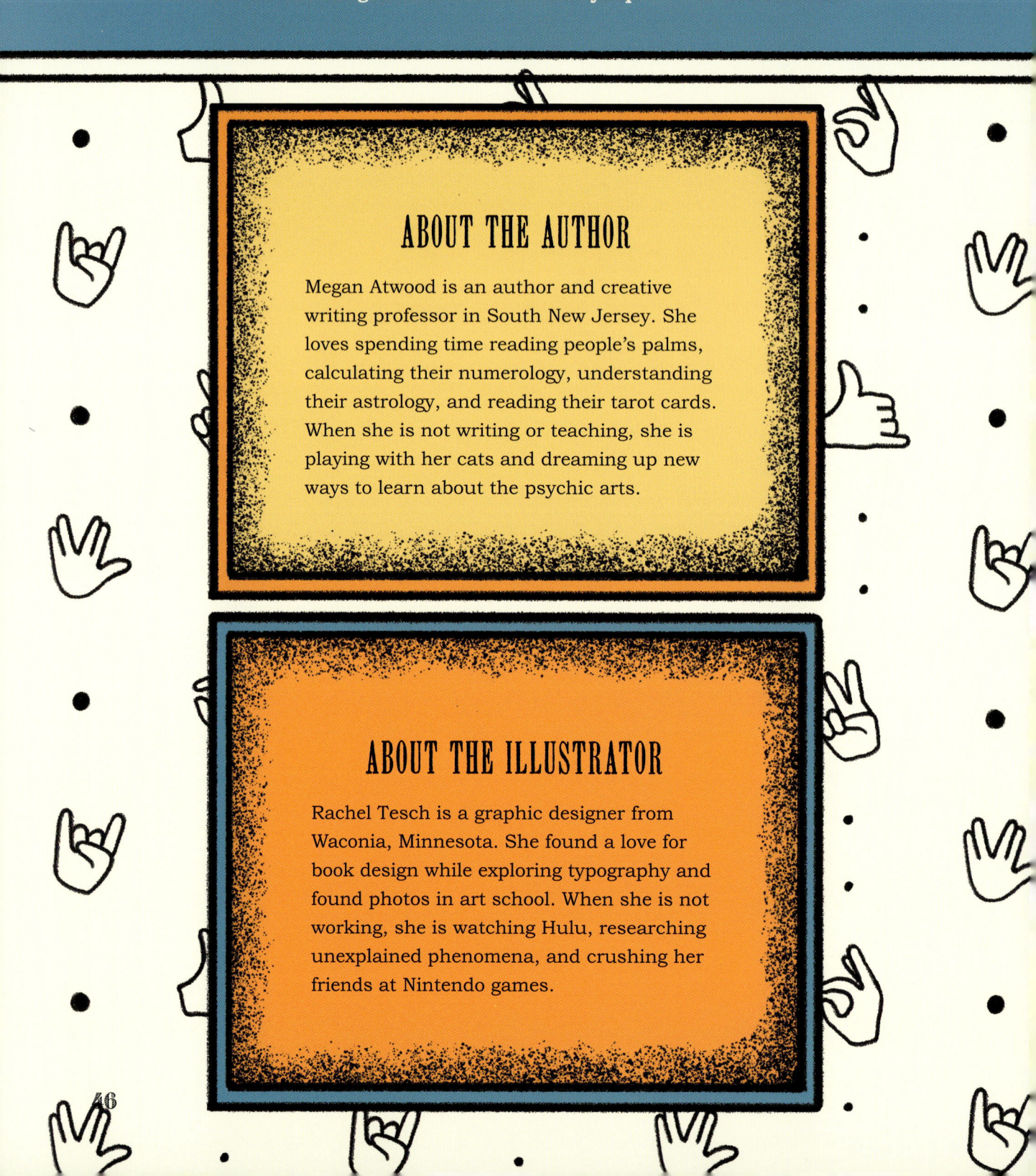

ABOUT THE AUTHOR

Megan Atwood is an author and creative writing professor in South New Jersey. She loves spending time reading people's palms, calculating their numerology, understanding their astrology, and reading their tarot cards. When she is not writing or teaching, she is playing with her cats and dreaming up new ways to learn about the psychic arts.

ABOUT THE ILLUSTRATOR

Rachel Tesch is a graphic designer from Waconia, Minnesota. She found a love for book design while exploring typography and found photos in art school. When she is not working, she is watching Hulu, researching unexplained phenomena, and crushing her friends at Nintendo games.

PALMISTRY GLOSSARY

celestial—relating to the stars and sky

divination—the act of telling the future

empathy—imagining how others feel

integral—essential to completeness

interpret—explain the meaning of; to conceive in the light of individual belief

karmic—referring to past lives or luck that results from actions, good or bad

ADDITIONAL RESOURCES

FURTHER READING

Have your parents or guardians check out these books for you!

Altman, Nathan. *Palmistry: The Universal Guide.* 2nd ed. New York: Guapo Publishing, 2017.

Mendoza, Staci. *The Art of Palm Reading: A Practical Guide to Character Analysis and Divination Through the Ancient Art of Palmistry.* Leicester, UK: Lorenz Books, 2014.

Southgate, Anna. *The Art of Palmistry: A Practical Guide to Reading Your Fortune.* New York: Sterling Ethos Publishing, 2016.

INTERNET SITES

Use FactHound to find Internet sites related to this book.

Visit *www.facthound.com*

Just type in 9780756561024 and go.

INDEX

accuracy, 12–13
air hands, 16
Apollo (Sun) mount, 24
Apollo line, 42

beginning steps, 44
bracelets, 42
broken lines, 34, 39, 41

chained lines, 31, 39
creative line, 42
crossbars, 39
crosses, 32, 34, 35
curved lines, 31, 34, 38

deep lines, 31, 32, 34, 38, 40, 41
double lines, 39, 41

earth hands, 17

fate (destiny) line, 35, 40–41
finger length, 12, 16, 17, 18, 19
fire hands, 19
forked lines, 31, 32, 34

gastromancy, 6
Guardian Angel line, 42

head line, 33–34, 41
heart line, 30–31, 33, 41
history, 9, 11

interpretation, 7
islands, 32

Jupiter mount, 22

left hand, 20
life line, 34, 38–39, 40, 42
Luna (Moon) mount, 27, 41

Mercury mount, 25
minor lines, 42
moleosophy, 6
mounts, 21–27, 41

negative readings, 7, 35

omphalomancy, 6
onychomancy, 6

party, 45–46
pedomancy, 6

right hand, 20
rules, 7

Saturn line, 40–41
Saturn mount, 23
shallow lines, 31, 32, 34, 37, 39
simian line, 42
squares, 32
stars, 32, 39
straight lines, 31, 34
success line, 42

triangles, 32, 39

Venus mount, 26

water hands, 18

DISCARD